Welcome to
The Giggle Club

The Giggle Club is a collection of new picture books made to put a giggle into early reading. There are funny stories about a contrary mouse, a dancing fox, a turtle with a trumpet, a pig with a ball, a hungry monster, a laughing lobster, an elephant who sneezes away the jungle and lots more! Each of these characters is a member of **The Giggle Club**, but anyone can join: just pick up a **Giggle Club** book, read it and get giggling!

Turn to the checklist on the inside back cover and tick off the Giggle Club books you have read.

TEE HEE!

HA HA!

To my brother
Jimmy
J.B.

First published 1996 by Walker Books Ltd
87 Vauxhall Walk, London SE11 5HJ

This edition published 1997

10 9 8 7 6 5 4 3 2 1

Text © 1996 Sam McBratney
Illustrations © 1996 Jill Barton

The right of Sam McBratney to be identified as author
of this work has been asserted by him in accordance
with the Copyright, Designs and Patents Act 1988

This book has been typeset in Souvenir

Printed in Hong Kong

British Library Cataloguing in Publication Data
A catalogue record for this book
is available from the British Library.

ISBN 0-7445-5282-6

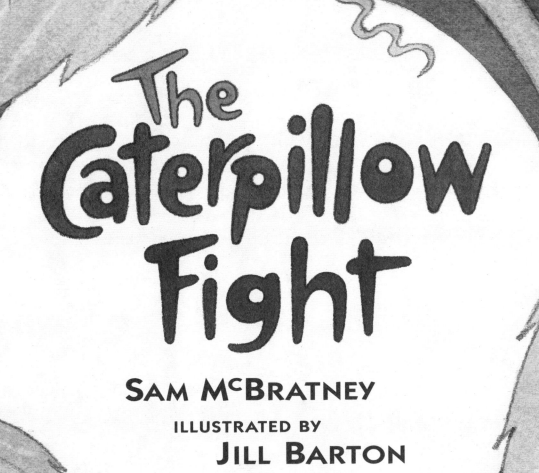

The Caterpillow Fight

Sam McBratney

ILLUSTRATED BY
Jill Barton

WALKER BOOKS
AND SUBSIDIARIES
LONDON · BOSTON · SYDNEY

When the caterpillars went
to their caterpillar beds,
They all had caterpillows
for their caterpillar heads.

One naughty caterpillar,
in the middle of the night,
Woke the other caterpillars
for a caterpillow fight.

Two little caterpillars
gave caterpillow blows
To another caterpillar
on her caterpillar nose.

The tallest caterpillar,
from her caterpillar height,
Brought down her caterpillow
with all her caterpillar might.

The other caterpillars,
hiding down below,
Watched the caterpillow
feathers fall like
caterpillow snow.

There were caterpillow thumps
and caterpillow whacks
On caterpillar tummies and
on caterpillar backs.
The caterpillar laughter
and the caterpillar din
Went on and on and on until ...

"Stop all this silly nonsense,
    I can hardly hear my ears.
This caterpillar laughing
    will end in caterpillar tears!"

Now when the caterpillars go
to their caterpillar beds,

There's just one *l-o-n-g* caterpillow
for all those caterpillar heads!